No Matter What

Jeff Rivera

Gumbo Entertainment Inc.

Prologue

"Don't be stupid, foo'."

Dio shot a look towards his homie, Spooky, who had his jacket clenched in his fist. He leaned back in the passenger seat of the '57 Chevy, swallowing.

Thunder rumbled and rain poured outside, making it impossible to see out the window. Storms scared Dio, always did, but his mind was set. He had to do this.

He pushed the door open and looked at the cathedral in front of him.

"Just keep the car runnin', *ése,*" he told Spooky.

Spooky was a big guy, tattoos up and down his arm. He normally would have stopped Dio easy, but tonight, nothing would stop him. Spooky, knowing this, just shook his head at Dio as he walked out the car.

Lightning illuminated the cathedral's majestic towers, shining off the stained glass windows. Dio had spent many a night imagining this as the place where, one day, he'd marry his lady Jennifer. He'd put everything into that dream. Now, as he yanked the heavy oak doors open, his heart pounded like a sub-woofer.

He stepped inside, trying to keep his shoes from squeaking on the old wood floor. The cathedral smelled like they never really cleaned the place, just painted over it.

The room was jam-packed with wedding guests listening to a children's choir sing, their voices echoing through the cathedral.

Dio, who had dressed in the best suit he could find, weaved in between the guests searching for a seat while trying to keep under the radar. He touched his chest, making sure the gun was still there. Yep, his .45 caliber felt like a brick inside that jacket pocket.

Where was she?

Jennifer once said she'd loved him since they were thirteen. They were both eighteen, now. She had taken care of Dio and believed in him when nobody else did. When his mother had threatened to send him away, she had taken him in. When he had nothing but Ramen noodles to eat, she fed him. When he'd gotten locked up in juvie the first time, she'd been there too. She promised she'd never leave him, not ever.

"*Estoy aqui para ti.* No matter what -- *siempre,*" they'd promised. And to Dio, a promise could never be broken.

He'd spent the entire year changing his life around just for her, so he could be the man she'd said she'd always wanted, so he could be the daddy his daughter needed. They were meant to be together and he was going to make Jennifer understand that. Even if it was the last thing he did.

He sat down in a pew as close to the front as he could without being detected. He wiped the sweat of his palms on his slacks as he sat. His breath was stifled and his throat was dry.

Here he was, in the church, about to... well. He just hoped that one day his little brother Daniel would understand. Maybe

4

one day he too would find a girl that meant the world to him, a girl he would kill for.

The music rose and all the heads in the chapel turned. Everyone gasped as Jennifer made her way down the aisle. She was breathtaking. It had been months since Dio had last seen her and she looked even better than he'd remembered. Olive-colored skin, full lips. She was the type of girl that never needed any makeup. In fact, she hated wearing it. Her dark brown hair was curled; glitter sparkled in it. She looked like an angel.

Her fiancé was a little older than her, a nice-looking black man who must have been rich, Dio thought. The one thing he could never give her. Jennifer lit up as she gazed at the other man, and Dio felt his heart break.

How could she do this to him? How could she throw away everything they'd had together?

Thunder rumbled outside but Dio's gaze never left Jennifer, even as the priest rambled on with the vows. His nose stung with unshed tears but he held them back. As the couple began their vows, his blood boiled.

"I, Jennifer Lalita Sanchez..." she said.

Dio swallowed around the lump in his throat. He couldn't believe his ears. His Jennifer was actually promising that punk her love.

Dio looked the other way, fighting back tears. He had to get a grip. Across the room, the creepy statue of Jesus glared back at him as if saying, "Don't do it."

He couldn't stand it anymore. His heart pounded as he reached for the .45 caliber in his pocket, his *cohete*. Rain pounded against the stained-glass windows and the roof.

He crossed himself, closed his eyes and prayed he was about to do the right thing.

Chapter 1

One year earlier

"You got cotton for brains or something? Move!" the drill instructor shouted as the group of guys stepped off the prison bus onto the hard desert ground.

He moved nose-to-nose with Dio. His breath smelled like cigarettes and garlic. Senior Jackson, they called him, a black boar of a man, sprayed spit with every syllable he spoke.

Dio had a pounding headache. Exhausted, hungry and aching inside, he closed his eyes and took a breath. His heart felt like it had been ripped out and stomped on. It'd been over three weeks since the accident. He didn't even know if Jennifer was dead or alive.

The lunatic drill instructor forced them to run five miles, screaming in their faces every step of the way.

Dio just wanted to be away from this place, chilling with his homies, smoking bud, bumping the oldies, but more than that, he wanted to be with his lady. They called him Playboy on the streets cause with his long hair and good looks all the ladies loved him, but truth was, Dio only had one girl in his heart: Jennifer.

She was by far the best thing that had ever happened to him. They'd met when they were just thirteen at Clark Middle School in Las Vegas. And it was like they'd known each other forever.

∞

"You're not too bright, are you kid?" Dio remembered his 7th grade language arts teacher, Mr. O'Donnell asking. He sunk in his chair as the class laughed in his face. He only wanted to know what a pioneer was. He didn't think it was such a stupid question.

"Should we send you to ESL?" O'Donnell asked.

The class roared with laughter.

Dio cringed. It wasn't like he wasn't trying. He just couldn't concentrate. Everything on the chalkboard looked like Chinese to him. He needed help but Mr. O'Donnell made him feel like scum every time he had a question.

He had too many problems at home to focus on schoolwork anyway. An alcoholic mom, bruises from her hand that he had to hide, no food in the fridge, and a little brother he was doing his best to protect.

On top of that, Dio was practically the only Mexican in the class, except for the skinny, nerdy little girl named Jennifer that nobody paid any attention to. Dio alone had to put up with all the smack and racist remarks.

The others didn't know what it was like being judged just 'cause of the color of their skin. Or being followed around a store just 'cause people automatically thought they were going to steal stuff, or having people lock their car doors when they crossed the street.

Ridiculous.

Sure, he had a temper sometimes but it wasn't always his fault. Truth was, he wanted nothing more than to bust these other kids' heads open for laughing at him but he needed to stay in school. Free lunch was the only way he could bring home enough for his brother, Daniel and mom to eat.

"Are you listening?" O'Donnell said. "Maybe we ought to knock you back to the 6th grade. Maybe the 4th grade for that matter."

The kids busted out laughing and O'Donnell shook his head, rummaging through his paperwork.

Dio squinted his eyes as fire began burning in the pit of his stomach. His nose flared.

Then Dio swore he saw O'Donnell mouth the word, "Mexicans."

What happened next, he didn't quite remember. But when he came to, Mr.

O'Donnell was on the floor holding a bloody nose. The next thing he knew, Dio was in the principal's office being screamed at.

"We do whatever we can to accommodate you people in our classes!" the principal shouted.

Dio stared at the floor, biting his nails.

This was it. He was going to get kicked out of another school again, and this time, there were no more options. He'd end up a dropout. Without an education, he was going to end up flipping burgers for the rest of his life and he'd never get any of his dreams accomplished. He'd become the very thing people assumed he would.

"It's not his fault," said a squeaky voice. It was Jennifer, pushing her glasses up her nose as she stepped into the principal's office.

"Excuse me?" the principal said.

"I wanted to punch Mr. O'Donnell myself," Jennifer said.

Dio blinked and a smile curved on his face. Little girl had *cojones*. Even when the principal began yelling at her, she didn't back down. Instead she fought back, mouthing off and telling him the school was going to be sued for discrimination.

Before long, they were both suspended. It was better than being expelled. Dio had never really had anybody stick up for him before. Jennifer had never spoken to him before. In fact, he couldn't remember her ever saying anything to anyone.

They sat outside the Principal's office for an hour, while Mr. O'Donnell was being shouted at for his "inappropriate behavior."

Dio gave Jennifer daps.

"*La Raza*," he said, trying to keep it cool.

She smiled.

From that day on, Dio and Jennifer had become best friends. They were inseparable. Besides his boys, she was the only real friend he had. Like him, she had a hard life, and when things got bad, they'd hide in her tree house and eat Rolo's chocolates. She'd sing to him with the most beautiful voice and they'd talk about their dreams of making it out of the barrio.

But then they were separated. Dio's mother kicked him out of the house for sticking up for his little brother when she went into another one of her drunken rages and he was lost in the foster care system until he was seventeen, bounced from home to home. He thought he'd never see Jennifer again.

Then, just months ago, they had been reunited. They picked up where they left off, only this time, they fell in love.

Gone was the skinny nerdy girl he remembered. Gone were the glasses. No, Jennifer was hot now. She'd filled out in all the right places, started wearing contacts and was the most beautiful girl he'd ever seen in his life.

∞

Now, as the drill instructor forced the prisoners to run around the boot camp like mules, it drove Dio *loco* not knowing if she was okay.

There had been an accident, a really bad one, and it was Dio's fault. He didn't know if Jennifer was alive or dead, his mind was going crazy, and now he had this insane man barking orders at them like he was their daddy or something. Dio could tell nobody said, "No" to Senior Jackson unless they wanted to get their butt kicked.

"Halt!" the drill instructor yelled.

Most of the trainees didn't have a clue what he meant but they figured he must be telling them to stop.

Thank God. Maybe now I can rest, Dio thought.

He felt like his stomach, lungs and everything else would come spewing out of his mouth at any moment. The only one who looked more pitiful than him was this skinny mulatto kid that Jackson called Simon. He wondered how the kid managed to look at himself in the mirror every day. Yeah, it was that bad. Coke-bottle glasses and more zits than Dio had ever seen on one person.

"Stand up, trainee," Jackson told Dio, flipping through his clipboard as Dio keeled over catching his breath.

"I can't," Dio said.

"I? Who is I? You're... Trainee Radigez. Get up, now!"

"Hold up, a'ight? Jeez." Dio said. The words came out of his mouth before he realized the big mistake he'd just made. Jackson came at him like a semi.

"Who the hell do you think you're talking to, boy? What's the third general rule from your manual?"

Dio was supposed to have memorized some fifty page manual with all these ridiculous rules. But that was the last thing that was on his mind.

"I don't know," Dio responded, smacking his lips. "You tell me."

"You're cruisin' for a brusin' aren't you, Trainee? 'Sir, Trainee Radigez doesn't know, Senior Jackson, sir!' That's what you say!"

"Sir, Trainee Rodríguez don't know, Senior Jack-Up, sir," Dio answered back. He could feel the stares of the other trainees. He hated when people stared at him.

"You a slow learner, Radigez?" Jackson asked, shoving his finger at Dio's head. "Think, Trainee, think!"

If he touches me one more time...

"It's Rodríguez, not Radigez," Dio spat back.

Jackson stepped even closer to him. "You correcting me, boy? You don't eat, sleep, or breathe unless I tell you to. You hear?"

Dio smacked his lips.

"Whatever," he mouthed.

Before Jackson could say more, an ugly mutt came out of nowhere and moved right up to Jackson's side. It growled and barked. Jackson smiled, patting it on the side. The dog looked like someone had run over it with a car several times, put it through the spin

12

cycle in a washing machine, then hit it with an ugly stick.

"Cool it, squad. This is Coffee and she don't take no smack from nobody. Now, listen up. You got three levels to get past in this camp and half of you won't make it past the first. If there's one thing I can't stand, it's dummies. And this squad is full of them. Some more than others," he said, looking directly at Dio. "And now, I'm going to work the dummy right out of you. Hit dirt and give me fifty. Now!"

They dropped to give him his pushups. Dio couldn't believe it. *More? Couldn't he see they were exhausted?*

"There is no fun here," Jackson continued pacing back and forth with Coffee trailing behind, "If you're not working, you're in school studying. And every night if you're not in your bunks sleeping, you're reading the general rules or the dictionary. The next time you don't know a word, look it up. Do I make myself clear, trainees?"

They stuttered, then said, "Sir, yes sir!"

"Sound like a bunch of losers. Are you a bunch of losers, Trainee Grossaint?" he stopped in front of a white kid with ice-blue eyes and chiseled features, diligently doing pushups as if he were reading a book.

"Sir, no sir," he responded.

"You sure about that, Grossaint? 'Cause it don't sound like it."

Dio felt as if he was going to cough up his lungs at any moment. His body quivered with each pushup. He still had forty-five to go.

Jackson got in his face, "That's not even a girl pushup."

The mutt barked in Dio's face and the trainees chuckled, which only burned Dio up more. He loved dogs but *they were about to find a missing dog somewhere if she kept it up.*

"Put some effort into it. My dead grandma could do a better job!" Jackson announced.

"I'm ... Trainee Rodríguez is trying, sir." Dio answered.

"Trying? You either do it or you don't. You are a pathetic excuse for a boy." Jackson stuck his weathered boots under Dio's chin. "When your chin hits these boots, then that's a pushup. Start over. One ... two..."

Now, it could have been the dung smell of Jackson's boots; who knows? But when it happened, Dio never felt more embarrassed in his life.

His last meal and everything else poured out of his mouth in chunks right on Jackson's boots.

"What the ...? Grossaint, get over here," Jackson yelled, restraining Coffee from licking his boots.

Grossaint hustled over to his side. "Sir, yes sir!"

"This look like puke to you, Grossaint? Why is there puke on my boots?"

"Sir, cause Trainee Radigez-"

"No, no and no! There's puke on my boots 'cause you haven't cleaned it off yet. Do it, now!"

Grossaint dropped to his knees. "Sir, how-?"

"Use your shirt, dummy," Jackson answered. Grossaint grimaced but scurried after Jackson on his knees, cleaning the vomit off as he approached Dio.

Dio was beyond embarrassed but kept his tough facade as Jackson stood nose-to-nose with him and whispered, "How do you feel now, Radigez?"

All that could be heard was the trainees breathing and Grossaint scrubbing Jackson's boots. Jackson's dark eyes peered right through Dio's soul, but he lifted his chin defiantly.

"Sir, fine. Feeling fine now, sir," Dio answered.

"One way or another, you're going to learn. I will win. I always do," Jackson said cracking a smile. Then he resumed his normal top-of-his lungs voice. "And since Trainee Radigez is *so* tired, you're all going to run for him. Five more miles!"

The other guys glared at Dio. "Sir, yes sir!" they answered.

"You just sit there and relax, Radigez. Don't worry," he said with a crafty smile, "They'll take care of everything."

Coffee barked in agreement.

Chapter 2

Dio was beat by the time they got into their large tent, where they had nothing but hard as rock bunks on the cold desert ground. Dio had slept on floors more comfortable.

Nothing's colder than winter in Las Vegas; the type that clings to your bones. It was even colder for Dio right now since the drill instructors had shaved off five years of his long locks.

He wasn't about to give them the pleasure of seeing how the haircut was tearing him apart. The icy breeze flowed over his bald head with every step he took.

Everyone in the squad avoided him and those that did look his way only glared.

Whatever. He didn't need them. He didn't need anybody. Still, it was times like these, he wished he was lying next to Jennifer. He thought about how they'd be whispering and laughing all night long, knowing if her parents ever found out he had snuck in, they'd have him arrested. They always hated him, but Jennifer saw past his long hair and tattoos. She never laughed when he said he wanted to get out of the gang and make something of himself.

They both had dreams and they were the only ones that could confide in each other about them. He thought they'd be together forever.

Grossaint's ice-blue eyes followed him as he tried to pull back the paper thin sheets.

He'd only been in camp a few days and already he'd made enemies. One of Grossaint's friends, Trainee Franklin, they called him, whispered something. Dio imagined it couldn't be a good thing.

He wanted to teach them some respect but he was too tired. He tossed and turned, switching the so-called pillow over.

He wanted to be near Jennifer so badly. She was the only thing that kept him sane. If he could just get to a phone, just for five minutes. He needed to hear her voice again.

His mind trailed off, and he was about to doze off when the whimpering and sobbing began.

"Shut up!" the trainees yelled. It was Simon.

What was he crying about? Dio wondered.

Simon went on like that all night long and just as Dio was about to sleep, Senior Jackson was in his face screaming, "Rise and shine, Radigez!"

Chapter 3

Dio felt stuck in a never-ending gym hell. One hundred pushups, two hundred sit-ups, two miles of running and whatever else Jackson could think up every morning. Then Jackson demanded they clean the walls, ceilings, floors, the cracks and corners all with a tooth brush.

With Coffee tracking dirt in and out of the hall, leaving "gifts" all over the place, it didn't make it any easier.

"I want to see myself in the reflection," Jackson said, pointing to the floors.

Dio's knees were raw from scrubbing the floor, his neck was throbbing, but all he could think about was Jennifer. Jackson was about to step away when Dio mustered up the courage to ask, "Um ... Sir, Trainee Rodríguez requests permission to speak, sir."

"What?" Jackson spat.

"Sir, Trainee Rodríguez was wondering if he could ... use the phone for a minute or two, sir."

Jackson laughed in his face. "You are asking me for a favor, Radigez?"

"Sir, Trainee Rodríguez's girlfriend is in the hospital, sir." His voice cracked with emotion.

"No!" Jackson bellowed. "You want phone privileges, you gotta earn them."

With that, Jackson kicked a dirty pail over and splashed it on the walls.

"Do it over. Mess up one more time, Radigez, and I'll make you wish you were never born."

As Dio set to work again, his nose stinging, Grossaint crawled up next to him, careful the junior drill instructor didn't spot him.

"He's a jerk," Grossaint said. It was the first time he'd ever said anything to Dio and he didn't know what to make of it.

18

"We should be able to use the phone anytime we want," he added.

"Yeah, it's our right," his friend Franklin agreed.

Was Grossaint actually trying to make friends? Maybe he wasn't as bad of a guy as Dio had thought.

"*Simón,*" Dio whispered, nodding in agreement.

Grossaint nodded toward Jackson's office. The door was slightly open.

"Just use the phone quick. We got your back," Grossaint eyed the junior officer, stepping away. "Go now, before he gets back."

"Yeah, we've got your back," Franklin said.

Grossaint and Franklin were right. If he was going to do it, now was the time. Even if he got caught, they'd only make him do more pushups or something. Jennifer was worth the risk.

Dio slipped inside the office and Grossaint gave him a reassuring nod.

He grabbed the phone and yanked it under the desk with him. Heart pounding, he called 4-1-1 and then the hospital connected him to Jennifer's room.

He just needed to know, to hear her voice. She was his soul mate; the only one he had really left in the world. If anything ever happened to her, Dio would never forgive himself.

"Hello," Jennifer's voice was dry and weak.

He was like a little kid again, talking faster than his mind could keep up with. "Baby, you all right? I'm in this camp. This prison boot camp and they don't let me do nothing but I've been praying every night. You okay? I miss you so bad."

She didn't answer right away, which only made him more worried.

"Got shot," she said.

"I know baby, but stay strong. Okay?"

"Dio," whatever she had to say was painful, "You know I care for you, don't you? I mean, we'll always have a connection but ..."

"But what?"

She sounded like she was holding back the tears, "I can't live like this anymore, Dio. *Mi familia* is right. I've got to do better. You and me, it's over."

It felt like a truck had landed on his chest. He struggled for breath for a moment. Then he said, "Baby, we're soul mates. Don't do me like this."

There was a silence on the phone for what seemed like forever.

"Baby?" Dio said.

"Try to understand," she responded.

Click.

Dio rocked back on his heels. For the first time in his life, he didn't have a friend in the world. No one.

He was alone.

His nose pinched, he could feel the tears starting to well up but he wasn't about to punk out. Instead he punched a wall. He must be dreaming. Jennifer would never just drop him like a...

Suddenly Coffee was there, barking in his face.

"What are you doing in my office?" Jackson shouted, grabbing him by the collar and pulling him down the hall so fast he didn't know what hit him.

He looked back at Grossaint and Franklin. They were both smirking.

Chapter 4

Dio had never been in an adult prison before, let alone in what they called the "hole." It was solitary confinement, as dark as night, and for someone who still had nightmares about being locked in a toy box by his mother it was horrible. Dio remembered that day clearly. He was just thirteen.

"You stupid, stupid, stupid boy," his mom said. He looked away, but she had him cornered against the wall. He could smell the tequila on her breath.

"You're trying to break up this family, aren't you?"

"No," Dio said.

She slapped him across the face sharply. "Liar."

He bit his lip. She was mad at him because one of the teachers had seen one of the bruises she gave him and the burn scar she'd made on him from the iron.

"What did you tell that teacher? Tell me!" she screamed at the top of her lungs.

"Nothing."

She grabbed him by the chin and shoved his face back against the wall. "I don't let little liars in my house, Dio. You want to be on the street again tonight? Huh? Let those bums you hang out with take care of you. See if they want you. 'Cause I sure don't."

Dio's nose flared. "Good, 'cause I don't want you either. You're a horrible mother."

Her hand came across his face so fast he didn't know what hit him. She didn't let up, over and over and over again, until he was on the floor in a fetal position.

That was the night she made him sleep in the toy box again. It was either that or she'd do something awful to his little brother.

Dio only hoped Daniel wasn't going through the same thing now, without him there to protect the little boy. The worst part was that here, Dio had little to think of besides Jennifer's rejection. His pride said forget about her; that he didn't need her anymore, but the truth was he didn't want anybody else. Living without Jennifer was like living without a piece of his soul.

Grossaint was definitely going to get it, one way or another. After all, as Spooky always said, "They hit you, you gotta hit 'em worse."

Chapter 5

"What now?!" Louise, the boot camp's cook, cried as Dio came in. Then she looked at him and sighed. "Another trainee to babysit."

She looked like trailer trash, as far as Dio was concerned, with her stringy, badly permed hair, no makeup, a pruned-up, wrinkled face, and hardly any front teeth. Dio winced away from her as she led him to a mountain of dishes bigger than he'd ever seen before.

"Well, get at it," she said.

Dio sighed. The last thing he wanted to do was this kind of work. He'd hated seeing his mom come home exhausted after working as a janitor and dishwasher, Daniel crying because he was so hungry. It was hardly a wonder his mother would rather be in a drunken stupor most of the time.

That's what led Dio to "alternative means of income." What was the big deal about selling a little dope, if it was going to keep his mom from one more job and brother from going hungry? At least that's how he used to justify it. In reality, it was the last thing he wanted to do.

He wiped the steam off his sweaty brow and noticed Simon, the zit face kid from earlier, holding a broom, and gawking at him with his mouth wide open.

"Whatchew want, foo'?" Dio asked, "Yeah, just keep sweepin'."

Simon shuffled away and Dio shook his head.

It took him forever but he finally finished that mountain of dishes, wiped the sweat off his brow, and sighed with relief. At least now he could rest.

"Did I say you could take a break?" Louise asked, startling him as she came up from behind with an even bigger load of dishes for him. Then other trainees from the squad brought in load after load. It was going to be a long day.

Chapter 6

Dio was more than exhausted after all that work, but then Grossaint entered the tent. Dio's hands itched to break his nose.

Days in the hole. All that kitchen work. Getting his phone privileges revoked forever so he'd never be able to call Jennifer? It was all Grossaint's fault and he was going to make him pay for it.

"I'ma mess you up, homie," Dio threatened, moving toward him.

Grossaint cracked a smile; his cronies surrounded Dio.

"Stupid wetback," Grossaint snarled, looking at Franklin as they moved in on Dio.

Dio was ready to take them on when a high-pitched voice cried, "Leave him alone!'

Everyone looked around for the source of the sound, then snickered when they saw Simon. He trembled like a little boy who knew he had a whipping coming.

"Don't bother him," he squeaked.

Dio was shocked. This scrawny little thing was coming to his defense? What was he going to do, slap them to death?

"Shut up, Simon," Grossaint replied.

His boys laughed.

"You shut up," Simon answered. Then he shrank back like a turtle in his shell.

Grossaint was about to do something when Franklin yelled, "Officer on deck!"

Everyone scurried to their bunks as Jackson marched inside.

Jackson seemed to sense something was off and immediately went to what he thought had to be the source of the trouble. "Radigez, what's going on here?"

"Sir, nothing sir," Dio answered.

Jackson stared him up and down, then asked Simon swift as a sword, "That true?"

Simon swallowed hard. "Uh—"

"Sir, you got a phone call," a junior officer called.

Saved by the bell.

Everyone held their breath until he exited.

Dio knew he had to chill for now. Grossaint's revenge would have to come another night.

He lay in bed thinking about what Simon had done. There was a courage about him Dio liked, one that his best homies back home had.

He decided then to sit up and write Jennifer a letter. If he couldn't use the phone, hopefully he could get through to her that way.

He grabbed a pen and paper from the box in front of his bunk.

Dear Jennifer,

Every day I wake up in the middle of the night and mi corazon me duele, 'cause I know everything that happened to you is my fault. Please, don't let what other ~~foos~~ people say make you not want to be with me. If I could do it all over again I would but I can't.

You gotta understand what I've been going through too. Nobody would tell me if you was alive or dead or nothing. When I heard your voice on the phone I ~~almost cried~~ about broke down. I've been dying inside every night thinking about you.

Don't give up on me. You're the only one I got besides mi hermanito. When I get out things are going to be so much better. You'll see. Just give me another chance, I'll prove it to you. Estoy aqui para ti. No matter what siempre. Remember?

Chapter 7

The whole next day Jackson had them digging ditches. Why? Because he said it built indefatigability.

"Do you know what indefatigability is, Radigez?" he asked.

"Um ... muscles?" Dio answered.

"So, we got jokes, do we? No, no, and no!" Jackson responded, "Indefatigability is being seemingly incapable of being fatigued. You build stamina; you don't get so tired."

Well, whoo-dee-doo! Who cares? Dio thought.

An older squad of guys wearing all white passed by. They were in the last level, ready to graduate.

"What are you looking at?" Jackson asked, "Half you guys won't even make it past this level."

Dio just wanted to get out of camp. With any luck he would get a legitimate job doing something that would make Jennifer proud to be with him. He still hadn't heard back from her, even though it'd been weeks, but he just knew that if he could make it out of boot camp and get his life together, he could win her back.

Dio wiped his brow. It was winter in the desert, but during the day it was just as hot as anytime of the year.

He looked over his shoulder to see Simon struggling beside him.

"Hey," Dio called, careful nobody else could hear.

"We're not supposed to be talking," Simon whispered in his high-pitch nasal voice.

Dio smacked his lips, "That foo's not going to do nothing to me he ain't done already."

Simon's eyes lit up a bit.

"I appreciate you sticking up for me last night. It was coo'," Dio said. "It was stupid, but it was coo'."

A smile spread across Simon's face, "Thanks!"

"Shh," Dio cautioned. "So, what are you? Black, Iraqi or what?"

"My dad's black and my mom's Hispanic."

"For real? That almost makes us brothers."

"It does?" Simon asked with a smile.

"*Simón*. Us brownskins gotta stick together, *sabes*? *La Raza*, dawg. That's why you gotta help me get back to Grossaint somehow. Hey, whatchew in here for anyway?"

Dio thought he was too skinny to be in a gang, too prude to hotwire a car. Simon withdrew. Whatever he'd done, he was too ashamed to talk about it.

"Come on, foo'. You can tell me. I got in here for possession of a firearm. Wrong place, wrong time. Foo's tried to blast me in a drive-by but got my girl instead. It's a'ight. I'ma get out and me and her gonna get back together like nobody's business. *Órale*."

"*Órale*? I don't speak Spanish," Simon said.

Dio shook his head. "*Órale. Simón*. You know. That's like saying, 'That's live. That's money.'"

Simon still looked confused.

"You know, 'That's cool, dude.'"

The light bulb came on in his head and Simon smiled and nodded his head like a bobblehead doll.

"*Órale. Simón*," he repeated.

Chapter 8

Jackson always had some new brainiac idea and since it was Grossaint's birthday, everyone had to make him a gift. Dio thought he'd give him a birthday gift to remember for a long time.

For some strange reason, Jackson's dog Coffee had taken a liking to Grossaint. No matter how many times he pushed her away, threatened her, pulled her by the tail, she was completely in love with him.

So that day, Dio approached Grossaint as he ripped his gifts open. He glared at Dio handed his gift to him and opened the gift like it was a bomb. Seeing nothing more than a homemade card, he crumpled it in his hand, tossed it aside, and continued opening the other presents.

"Chow time!" a junior officer yelled.

Everyone got up, put their shoes on, and headed out.

When Grossaint did the same, however, his shoes squelched. He sat back down and pulled them off to find a funky smell and gush in his shoes, one of Coffee's "gifts".

"What the-" Grossaint exclaimed. Dio and Simon walked by him, trying not to laugh. Then Simon blew it by saying, "Happy birthday."

Dio nudged him. "Stupid. Keep it on the down-low."

Grossaint's teeth gritted, his face beet red with anger. Dio knew he was in for it, something big this time. It was no longer fun and games.

It was war.

Chapter 9

Dio couldn't open Jennifer's letter quick enough. He was supposed to be cleaning out the grease traps in the kitchen but instead stole a few minutes to read.

Dear Dio,

It took me a long time to write this letter because the medicine they put me on makes me sick to my stomach. You say you're sorry, you say you care for me pero no te creo. I think ~~you're selfish~~ all you think about is yourself.

You don't know what it's like to constantly have to defend you to all my friends. It's too much for me. They say the bullet almost hit mi corazon. I should have been dead but ~~an angel~~ someone's watching over me and I can only think it's like a second chance and I've got to do things right this time.

I want to believe this time it will be different, that you will change but everything you'd said you'd do, you haven't done. You said you'd quit banging, that you'd quit selling, that you'd ~~buy me a real engagement ring~~ and go back to school but I don't see any of that. When I see you in a tie and shirt and you've got a real job, then I'll believe you.

Jennifer

The letter tore Dio apart. Part of him was just glad she'd written back but he wanted so badly for her to forgive him. He knew what had happened was serious, that his past had caught up to both of them. And it's not that he was totally surprised by her

31

reaction but to hear her say things like this just hurt.

"Oh for heaven's sake!" Louise yelled from the other room. Dio shook his head and got up to go back to work. Then, he thought he heard a sniffle.

Frowning, he wiped his hands and followed the sound. Louise was standing in the pantry, her back turned and arms folded. Dio cleared his throat.

"You all right?"

"Mind your own business and get back to work," she snapped.

"Whatever," Dio said, turning to leave. Discomfort prickled over his skin. He hated to see a woman cry.

Then he thought of something. He left for a moment, heading outside to a nearby flower bed, and then returned to the pantry. Approaching Louise with caution as she sobbed, Dio set a violet down beside her. As he turned to leave, her voice stopped him.

"Hey, get over here," she said.

"Yeah?" he answered, turning around.

"You trying to be sweet to me or something? Whatchew want?" she asked, wiping her eyes.

"I don't want nothing," he said, smacking his lips.

She grunted. "Well, you ain't gonna get nothing out of it."

"Whatever," he said. It was probably just as hard for her to say, "Thank you" as it would be for him.

32

"I'm not trying to get up in your business or nothing but," he said, "what's the matter, anyway?"

"Don't get married, that's what's the matter," she said.

"Ah, relationships. I know how that goes," he said, leaning against a counter.

"What do you know about relationships?" she said, turning and putting her hands on her hips.

He bit his thumb nail and said, "Got female problems, that's what."

"What kind of female problems?"

"My girl's mad at me right now." He shrugged.

"She got a reason?"

Dio grunted. "I just want it to be like it used to."

Louise started putting things away again, her tears apparently gone. "Well, relationships fade," she said.

"Not me and Jennifer," he said, standing up straighter. "We're soul mates. We're just going through a bit of a rough patch."

Dio took the letter out of his pocket. "I know I'm not supposed to bring nothing to work but... she said it right here, in this letter. She don't want nothing to do with me. She don't know how much I love her. You're not gonna nark on me, are you?"

"Just read the darn letter," she grunted.

As Dio read it to her, she listened carefully. When he had finished, she laughed and went back to putting the cans in their spots. "Well, sounds like she still wants you to me."

"For real?" he asked, his eyebrows raising.

"Listen to what she's saying!"

When Dio frowned, Louise made an impatient noise, "Give me that," she said, snatching the letter from him. She began reading: "'When I see you in a tie and shirt and you've got a real job...' She wants you, but you gotta get it together. Isn't that what she's saying here?"

"For real?" he repeated, his eyes lighting up. "You think I've got a chance?"

"'For real'? Of course 'for real'. You're talking to a woman here." She laughed again. Then she turned serious, her eyes soft. "Listen, if you really love her, don't let her get away. Write her back. You still got a chance."

"What should I say?" he asked, stepping towards Louise with his fists clenched anxiously.

"You'll know," Louise answered. "You love her, after all."

Chapter 10

Dio thought long and hard about everything Louise had said as he sat on his bunk that night drawing a picture of Jennifer. Jennifer had always encouraged him to draw and she knew it was the one thing that he was passionate about. It allowed him to escape whatever he was going through at school or with his mom.

Now, as he traced the last details of his vision of Jennifer, he was lost in her, lost in what could be.

No matter how ticked off he felt sometimes about her trying to break up with him, he couldn't help himself. He was in love with her. And though he'd never tell Spooky or any of his boys back home, it was the truth. She was the only one for him. He wanted her and he was willing to fight for her.

He knew he couldn't procrastinate forever, drawing the same lines over and over again, so finally he decided to get to writing.

Dear Jennifer,

Sometimes the things I mean in my head don't exactly come out the way they're supposed to. You know if I was there right now, I'd be lying next to you, ~~hugging~~ holding you. I'd be stroking your pelo, kissing you, making you feel good. You know that's all I think about here, being with you. It's the only thing that gets me through ~~day~~ each day. My heart pounds every time they pass out the mail 'cause I'm hoping I'll get something from you.

That's what you do to me, baby. You make my heart pound. I know you're going to pull through in the hospital and when I get out things are going to be better ~~much better~~. You'll see.

Oh! I almost forgot. Don't know if you're feeling up to it or if the doctors will let you but visitor's day is coming up next Friday at 6pm. Think you can come?

Playboy

"Whatcha doing?" Simon asked then.

"You messin' my vibe, man," Dio snapped.

Simon backed away like he had just been slapped across the face, which only made Dio feel bad.

"I'm just writing my lady," Dio grunted, repositioning himself on his bunk.

"Can I see?" Simon asked, peering over Dio's shoulder.

"Man, don't you got no girl of your own? Jeez."

"No," Simon answered, staring at the dirt floor.

"Homie, you gotta learn to strut. You can't slump around all the time. How you expect to get no respect?"

"Yeah, listen to him. He'll teach you a thing or two," Grossaint called out, making everyone laugh.

"Foo'" Dio said, "I ain't in the mood for you."

Dio started for him but Coffee got up and started growling. Grossaint smiled at the dog. "Good girl."

Simon tugged at Dio. "It's not worth it. They'll just send you back to the hole. Think about your girl."

Dio hated to admit it but Simon was right.

"You think you're so smart but you're in camp just like the rest of us," Dio said to Grossaint as he backed away.

"At least I'm going somewhere when I get out. You'll just be stuck in the ghetto," Grossaint responded.

Dio smacked his lips, "Foo', soon as I get out, I'ma be an artist with my own car design shop."

Grossaint snorted. "You're dreaming."

"Yeah?" Dio challenged. "At least I'm not going back to the trailer park with my Ma and Pa and girlfriend. I mean, sister."

The squad busted out laughing, which took Dio by surprise .

"I gotta girl at home," Grossaint said, pulling himself up, "and at least she ain't some dumb street rat like yours."

"Oooh," the guys groaned as one, looking on eagerly.

"Yeah? Least she ain't as dumb as your mama. Your mama so dumb if she spoke her mind, she'd be speechless."

The guys busted out laughing.

"Your mama so dumb," Dio continued, "Wait ... she had you."

Everyone roared in laughter. Dio had a whole bunch of "Yo' Mama" jokes lined up for Grossaint but he could see he'd struck a chord in him. So he didn't bother to push it anymore, not today.

Chapter 11

Dio stayed up the whole night before that Friday's Visitor's Day thinking about seeing Jennifer again. He hadn't gotten a letter back from her yet, but he knew Jennifer. She'd get mad at things, but she got over them. He figured she'd definitely show up one way or another.

But the next day in the visitor's room, he waited until no other trainees were left except him and Simon.

"Where's your girl, Dio?" Simon finally asked.

"She'll be here. You'll see..." Dio answered, not wanting to look at him. "Where's your mom and dad?"

Simon shrugged.

"They just missing out," Dio said.

Simon sniffled. "Yeah."

"Who needs them? They don't show up, you don't want them to show up," Dio added.

Simon's eyes watered. "Yeah. I gotta go to the bathroom."

Simon trailed off to ask Jackson to use the head.

Poor kid, Dio thought. *What parent wouldn't want a kid like that?*

As the hour progressed, the other trainees' guests came and went. Even Grossaint had a guest, some big guy that looked like he could have been his brother.

Finally, there were no guests left and Dio was left completely embarrassed. The squad gave him a "you-didn't-get-anybody-to-visit-you?" look while they lined up waiting for Jackson to give them permission to go. He kept his chin up, looking straight ahead, but his pride was crumbling.

Jackson came up to him and spoke in a low tone. "Where's this lady friend of yours you were talking about?"

Dio frowned, clenching his fists.

Chapter 12

It had been three weeks since he had heard from Jennifer. Was she trying to forget him? It wasn't like her to do something like this. Yeah, maybe he'd messed up real bad but she had to know he'd do anything for her.

He felt like he was just going through the motions at boot camp. Why even try that hard? What good was life without Jennifer?

Nothing was more obnoxious than those obstacle courses Jackson made them do. They were supposed to be making some improvement each time but Dio didn't get the whole point.

To be honest, he barely tried. He just needed to stay under the radar long enough to graduate from camp in a few months and get out.

"Chow time," Jackson announced to the exhausted trainees.

Excitement spread among them as they lined up for food. It was about time, as far as Dio was concerned. He was starving to death and couldn't wait to eat.

"Go ahead everyone! Except you, Radigez."

Dio froze. *Now what?*

"Sir?" Dio said, staying where he was put.

"Get over here. What do you think you're doing today? My dead grandmother could do a better job."

"Sir, Trainee Rodríguez is just doing what you told him, sir."

"No, no, and no! Need I remind you, if I don't see any improvement, your sentence will be extended."

Dio sighed, muttering something under his breath.

Jackson charged into his face. "What'd you say? What's the tenth general rule?"

"Sir, all trainees must do their very best but Trainee Rodríguez was doing his best, sir."

"Your best? That was your best? You want to ever see that girl of yours again or what?"

"Sir, 'course I ... Trainee Rodríguez does, sir."

"Hit dirt and give me one hundred."

"Sir?"

There was no way it was physically possible. He was exhausted from everything Jackson had made them do before.

"Hit dirt and give me two hundred, then," Jackson challenged.

Dio was furious but began pounding out the pushups before Jackson added more.

He kept Dio at it: sit-ups, squats, anything he could think of until every vein in Dio's neck was strained.

"You keep talking about this girl you want to see," Jackson said, pacing back and forth as Dio kept going. "You think she wants some street bum that can't get a job, in and out of jail, some quitter?"

"Sir, no sir," he answered, barely able to catch his breath.

"Give me a hundred more pushups."

"Sir, I ... sir, Trainee Rodríguez can't, sir. I'm sorry but it's impossible."

"Impossible? Can't? Them words ain't words in my camp, only assiduity. What's assiduity, Trainee?"

"Sir ... Trainee Rodríguez doesn't know, sir," he answered. His arms were shaking and his body aching and he certainly wasn't in the mood for vocabulary lessons.

"Look it up sometime. You're going to need it." Then Jackson snorted. "Fine. Go and quit. See if your girl wants some quitter. Yeah, that's going to happen."

He shook his head and walked away.

He watched him go and something struck inside. Another person giving up on him, another person not believing in him. That man didn't know half of what he was capable of, Dio thought. He was going to show him.

Nobody called him a quitter.

Dio got down on the ground and cranked out those pushups.

Jackson raised an eyebrow as Dio hopped up and stood at attention, catching his breath. "Sir, Trainee Rodríguez is finished, sir."

Jackson could hardly hide his smile.

"All right. You get on inside. And you better wash up before you eat. Nothing's worse than smelling sweaty nasty funk."

After that, Jackson was so proud, though he'd never admit it, that he even arranged for Dio to get an extra spam burger.

Chapter 13

Dio's bunk had never felt so good as that night. He was so tired he couldn't even think.

But a warm smile spread over his face as he realized what he had done. He'd actually succeeded at something.

He knew Jennifer would have been proud. She always said he had so much potential. Somehow, in his own weird way, he felt he was one step closer to becoming somebody. He didn't know who or what yet, but someone better, someone stronger.

From that point on, every night before he said his prayers and went to bed, he read the dictionary, learning new words so he could keep up with Jackson.

"Rise and shine, Radigez!" Jackson yelled in Dio's face the next morning. His body felt like an old truck that needed to be warmed up. But he managed to get up, a new fire pushing through him.

He wasn't a quitter anymore.

Chapter 14

Dio had been so busy at camp, trying to improve, that he was surprised when Jennifer's letter came in two weeks later. Before he could even open it, Simon was at his side.

Dio tried to hide his smile. "Just hold up, ése."

He tore the letter open, crossed himself and said a little prayer. Then he began reading aloud to Simon.

Dear Dio,

The picture you drew of me was really sweet. You're so talented. Sorry I didn't make it to your visitor's day. I had to go back into the hospital for internal bleeding. It's ~~a trip~~ funny, this whole thing has brought mi familia together again. They want me to come home, Dio. Can you believe it? I almost cried when my mom said that. You know your padres care, sabes? But sometimes you just need to hear it from them.

"I know how that goes," Simon added.

Dio blinked and then noticed everyone in the squad was perched at the edge of their seats, listening. He felt completely exposed but kept reading anyway.

I'm kind of worried because I don't want no problems like we had before. I don't want all the gritos. Maybe things will change. I hope so cause I don't ~~want to run away again~~ have no other place to go. I told you my big dreams, Dio. I believe in them still, I do. It's just I get tired of depending on other people. I want to go to school again. I want to be somebody. I never told my mom what I did out there to survive when I ran away. It'd break their heart.

"What'd she do?" Simon asked.

Dio's heart jumped to his throat.

"Yeah," Grossaint said, winking at Dio, "what *did* she do?"

Everybody busted out laughing. Dio was about to pound Grossaint when Jackson entered.

Dio didn't want to think about what Jennifer told him she'd had to do to survive. He never judged her and she never judged him and he guessed that was why they could tell each other everything. Nobody else seemed to understand what it was like going through the things they did. That's why it felt so good to have someone like her in his life that knew the whole story.

"Everyone, let's go!" Jackson said.

Now where are we going? he wondered as Jackson led them to a big wooden trailer-like building, a hooch. Was it another surprise exercise routine? Were they in trouble? Had Grossaint finally told on him about the whole birthday surprise he'd left in his shoes the while back?

It was pitch-dark inside but as Jackson flicked the light on, Dio could see it was jam-packed with bunks. A smile spread across Dio's face as he realized what was happening.

They had just moved up the next level in the squad. As they opened the boxes with their striped clothes, the squad could hardly contain their excitement.

Dio was one step closer to graduating, and one step closer to Jennifer.

Chapter 15

"Of course, she wrote back. I told you I knew what I was talking about," Louise said, wiping her brow.

Dio was practically hopping with excitement.

"I started writing her back. Wanna hear it?"

"Go ahead. But hurry up. You've got work to do," she said, smiling slightly as she stirred the pot of soup.

"Yes, ma'am," Dio said. Then he cleared his throat.

Dear Jennifer,
Today I had to help the squad out.

"Wait—Wait—Wait! Is that how you're going to start out the letter?" Louise asked.

"Well, yeah. Why not?" he said, raising his eyebrow

"Hmm," she said, adding more salt to her soup.

"What's wrong with it?"

She put the wooden spoon down, "Well, you're talking about *yourself*, Dio. What about how she's feeling? A woman wants to know you care, that you're making her feel number one. You wanna win this girl back for good, you gotta put her first and that's starts with that letter."

Dio thought for a while. She was right. He guessed sometimes he came across kind of selfish. So, after a few minutes of thinking, he read Louise what he'd written.

Hey Baby,

Thanks for the compliments. Glad you're feeling better. Hope things get much better with your parents. Wish I could say the same for my moms. ~~She's a b~~ You're lucky. I believe in your dreams too, mija. I know it. You're going to be big and I'm gonna buy all your rolas.

You and me gonna be together again real soon. First thing I get out I'ma get us a place together. I got it all planned out. They say I'll be able to get my GED by the time I graduate boot camp. Been studying day and night, even reading the dictionary like nobody's business. ~~It's boring but~~ Can you believe it? Ain't that a trip? And to think the teachers in school used to say I'd never graduate. Anyway, miss you mucho. Te amo.

Playboy

Louise nodded, but her mind was elsewhere. "What do you mean the teachers used to say you'd never graduate? They told you you were stupid or something?"

"Pretty much," Dio answered, scrunching his mouth.

"What did your mom say?" she said, putting her hands on her hips.

His mind flashed back to all drunken abuse from his mother and he just shrugged. She'd called him much more than "stupid".

"Jennifer was the only one back then that would say anything good," he replied. "I was thirteen and I was going to commit suicide. For real."

"At thirteen?"

He looked away from her biting his lips. Truth was, he wasn't joking. It really was that bad. If it hadn't been for Jennifer and the fact that Daniel needed him, he didn't know where he'd be.

"Let's talk about something else. 'Kay?" he said.

"Can I just ask you one thing about that, Dio? Where's your mom now?"

"Who cares? Probably rehab again."

"Drugs?"

"Booze. Just hope *mi hermanito's* okay. I don't want him getting in no foster care like I had to."

Louise shook her head. "Yep," Dio smiled. "Me and my brother's all tight. One day, me and Jennifer gonna get enough money together to take care of him and her little sister too."

"Sounds like a great girl, Jennifer. Dio, do me a favor, you get her back, hold on to her and never let her go. You hear?" She put her hand on his shoulder, looking right into his eyes.

"Yes, ma'am," he replied, biting the inside of his cheek.

Chapter 16

"Get a move on!" Jackson roared as the squad ran in the scorching desert sun.

Dio had never run faster in his life. He was dripping with sweat and the desert sucked his throat dry but it felt good.

Grossaint and him were head-to-head at the last wall in the obstacle course then up the thick rope—one hand over the other, until Dio touched the top and slid down just as Grossaint was halfway up.

Dio even gave him a wink on the way down and raced to the finish line. Jackson clicked his stopwatch. "9:03."

The squad cheered Dio.

Jackson cleared his throat. "All right. Don't get too excited. Not bad, Radigez. Not bad."

Grossaint raced up to Jackson.

"9:47," he called, checking his stopwatch.

"Sir, Trainee Grossaint requests permission to speak, sir," he asked Jackson.

"Go ahead," Jackson grunted.

"Sir, Trainee Radigez didn't touch the top of the rope all the way. He's supposed to—"

"Trainee, what's the ninth general rule?"

"Um ... Sir, trainees must focus on their own excellence but-"

"Stop being petulant. What is petulant, Grossaint?" Jackson barked.

Grossaint looked at him, dumbfounded. "Sir, I—"

"No, no and no! Not, 'Sir, I'. What is it, Grossaint? Haven't you've been doing your studies?"

"Sir, yes, sir. But—" Grossaint stuttered.

"Sir, Trainee Rodríguez requests permission to speak, sir." Dio announced.

"Go ahead." Jackson said, sounding exasperated.

"Sir, petulant is an adjective meaning moody, ill-tempered and whiny."

"That is correct, Trainee," Jackson said with a surprised smile, "You know, Grossaint, you ought to follow Trainee Radigez's lead and get to your studies."

"But-" Grossaint started until Jackson held up his hand.

"There are no excuses in life, Grossaint."

Dio smiled at Grossaint and said just loud enough so only he could hear it, "Yeah, there are no excuses in life, Grossaint."

Chapter 17

"Heeey, Simon," Grossaint said as the squad worked out in the camp's garden the next day.

Everyone laughed as Grossaint sashayed in front of them. Dio watched Simon shrink into his shell and nudged him.

"Say something. Why do you let that fool knock you like that, homes? Gotta stick up for yourself."

Grossaint puckered his lips at Simon. "Simon!"

Everyone busted out laughing.

Dio rose. "Shut up, Grossaint. Unless you like walking around like that."

Grossaint burned red. "What's up with you and him anyway?"

"You're just ticked cause I kicked your butt on the course ... again," Dio said.

The squad laughed.

"Whatever, stupid," Grossaint grumbled.

"I know you are but what am I?" Simon cried.

Everyone froze. *Oh, my god. What a nerd,* Dio thought. He shook his head, embarrassed for Simon.

"Sticks and stones, homie," Simon added, "Sticks and stones!"

Dio called Simon through gritted teeth, "Shut up."

Simon stared at him. "What'd I say?"

Grossaint laughed. "Loser."

Everyone roared with laughter and Simon shrank back into his shell.

Dio waited until everyone was gone and then said, "*Chale*, homes. You can't let him walk all over you like that. You gotta fight."

"I don't know how."

Dio looked to see if anyone was watching then pulled Simon inside one of the laundry buildings. He started throwing punches into the air.

Simon winced.

"E*se,* don't back up like that. You gotta fight back. Hold up your fists."

Dio showed him how to hold them, how to jab, how to duck but he wasn't getting it right.

Finally, Dio sighed. "Look, you gotta jab," Dio said, throwing a punch at the wall. "You gotta—" But his fist went right through the plaster wall. Simon gasped.

"My bad," Dio said, cracking a smile.

The hole in the wall was big enough to see right through outside.

"Senior Jackson wants us to head out," Grossaint said from behind them. He smiled and then turned to leave.

"He's going to tell. He's going to tell!" Simon whispered.

"Chill. I'll handle it," Dio said, though he was just as nervous.

But Grossaint said nothing that day, and not the next either.

Chapter 18

Something was wrong; Dio couldn't put his finger on it. Another month had passed and he had been working his butt off to keep up with his homework, to do all the chores with Louise and complete his training, but it wasn't getting him any closer to Jennifer.

He was liking who he was becoming and all but he was starting to wonder if it was worth it. And then there was the whole Grossaint situation.

Grossaint still hadn't said anything about him punching a hole in the wall, but he didn't trust him. Dio was doing so well that he was promoted to supervise the rest of the squad and he knew Grossaint didn't like it one bit. Not only that but although Simon wouldn't talk about it, he knew Grossaint was still picking on him when Dio wasn't around. He couldn't always be there to protect Simon so whenever he got the chance, he tried to show him how to defend himself, how to strut, how to stand up tall and make people respect him.

In fact, Simon was starting to get some real *cojones*. He was like a little dog that would bark at all the big dogs, but only if his owner was around; otherwise Simon was defenseless.

Dio didn't mind sticking up for Simon, but he knew Simon had to learn to do things on his own. In just a few short months they were going to be graduating and they might never see each other again.

∞

"You get all that work done?" Jackson asked Dio one day as he tied another bag of laundry.

"Sir, yes, sir. Just have to finish one more bag."

"Good. Good. How's that girl of yours doing?" Jackson asked.

"Sir, she's all right, sir," Dio answered.

"Whatcha going to do when you get out?" Jackson asked.

Dio frowned. Jackson obviously wanted something, but he wasn't getting out with it. "Sir, get a job, I guess, sir. Provide for *mi amor.*"

"That's good. What kind of job you thinking about?"

"Sir, anything, to start. I'd love to have my own car design shop but—"

"Good. Well, if you're going to be an artist . . ."

Here come the lectures, Dio thought.

"...Don't let nobody stop you. Just make sure you get an education behind you. Tried to tell my son that."

"Sir, your son, sir?"

"Boy always had his head in the clouds." Jackson chuckled.

"Sir, what's he do now, sir?

"He don't do nothing. He's dead."

Dio didn't know how to respond. "Sir, how'd he die, sir?"

Jackson started to answer the question, then slipped back into his drill instructor role.

"Better get back to what you were doing," he said, changing the subject.

"Sir, yes, sir," Dio answered.

He watched Jackson make his way out of the laundry room. He always seemed like such a confident man, but now he looked lost and alone.

It was funny. A few months ago Dio couldn't stand anybody at the camp, and now, he hated to admit it, but the truth was, it was starting to feel like some of them were family.

Chapter 19

Grossaint looked like he was going to cry. Everyone did, really, as they stood in front of the main gate staring at Coffee's dead body. Somehow she had gotten out and been hit by a car. As much as Dio couldn't stand that bratty little dog, part of him had grown to love her, too.

"Well, we ought to get her off the road," Jackson said.

"Sir, Trainee Grossaint requests permission to speak, sir," the boy said, stepping up.

"Go ahead."

"Sir, how'd she get out, sir? We double-lock the gates all the time," Grossaint asked.

"Well, somebody was careless, that's for sure. Sometimes things happen, Grossaint. Come on, now; help me. Let's go."

They all put on latex gloves and lifted her.

"It's true," Simon told him, looking Grossaint straight in the eye as if he were threatening him. "Sometimes, things just happen."

Grossaint's nostrils flared. He didn't say a word but Dio sensed something was about to go down, something bad.

Chapter 20

Dio smiled as Jackson approached him in the laundry room. He knew he'd be proud of all the work Simon, him and the rest of the squad had done that day, and maybe he'd even let them off early. After all, he'd been lifting bags of laundry all day and was exhausted.

But then Dio's smile faded. Something was wrong.

Jackson had Grossaint by the neck, leading him toward Dio, followed by two junior officers. They all stopped in front of Dio.

"Show me where it is, Grossaint," Jackson commanded.

Grossaint brushed past Dio and pulled back a giant washer.

What is going on? Dio wondered.

Then he saw, clear as day, a giant hole in the wall directly behind it. Not the small hole that he had punched through, but instead, a hole big enough to crawl out of, leading directly out of the gates that locked them in. His mouth dropped.

"You do this, Radigez?"

"Sir, Trainee Rodríguez . . . yes, but no, not—"

Simon stepped in front of him. "Sir, it wasn't his—"

"Shut up, Simon," Jackson spat.

He stepped in front of Dio, nose-to-nose, and said in a low voice, "Now, I'm going to ask you again, did you do this or not, Radigez?"

"Sir, I . . . I . . . sir, no, sir," Dio stuttered.

"Sir, yes he did, sir," Grossaint answered. "I saw him."

"Sir, so did Trainee Franklin, sir," Franklin added. One by one, Grossaint's cronies said, "Sir, so did I, sir."

Dio felt like his world was closing in on him.

"Sir, it wasn't me, sir! It wasn't me, sir!" he pleaded.

Jackson shook his head. "Take him away."

Dio's eyes met Simon's as the junior officer took him away. He looked like a little lost puppy, with Grossaint and his boys circling him, ready to devour their prey.

Chapter 21

As if a week in the hole wasn't bad enough, when Dio did get out, they stripped him of his striped outfit and put him back in the dark clothes, the first level.

Dio didn't know how he'd be able to make it through everything all over again. His eyes burned with the thought that he wouldn't be able to see Jennifer anytime soon.

Every minute he was in camp was a minute she was slipping through his fingers.

He cradled himself in his bunk and sobbed. At first, as quietly as he could, but then it was uncontrollable. The new trainees yelled at him to shut up, but he couldn't help it.

He wished Jennifer was there to tell him that everything would be all right and that he'd make it through this.

They didn't even let him work in the kitchen anymore and he never got to explain to Louise what happened. He only hoped she wouldn't be disappointed in him.

Chapter 22

It had been a whole month. His birthday came and went, but still no word from Jennifer. He missed things the way they used to be.

∞

"I've only got fifteen minutes," Dio told Louise one day as she snuck him into the pantry where they could talk in private.

"How you holding up?" she asked.

Dio paced back and forth, breathing heavily.

"Hey, hey. Calm down," she said, holding up her hand.

He slammed his fist in the wall, feeling like he needed to be checked into a crazy house.

"Listen to me, Dio, calm down. Okay? The truth will come out in the end and if Grossaint really has done what you said he's done, karma will come back to him. I promise."

"Yeah, right," Dio said pacing back and forth, "And where's Jennifer? Huh? She said she'd never leave me, that we'd have each other's backs forever and she lied. She lied!"

"Listen, you need to understand things from her perspective. Maybe-"

"No! I'm sick of seeing things from her perspective. What about me? What about what I'm going through?"

Louise sighed and put her hands on his shoulders. "Okay, you know what you need to do? Write a letter to Jennifer. Say what you've always wanted to say, just let it all out. Put it in an envelope and seal it up. I mean, don't send it or anything but write it. I know it sounds like a bunch of bunk but I'm telling you, Dio, you'll be amazed how much tension that releases."

Dio sighed. He was tired of all these psychobabble tips. He just wanted Jennifer back.

"I know it's hard," Louise said to him, "but please try. Things always work out in the end."

"Yeah, right," he said and then left.

He felt bad about it later. He knew she was just trying to help and she didn't have to. Nobody was making her be his friend. So, he figured as soon as he got back to the hooch he'd grab some paper and pen and start writing that letter Louise was talking about. What harm could there be?

Dear Jennifer,

Why you ignoring my letters? You not the sweet girl I knew. You probably got a sancho on the side when we were going out. You just cold. I'm sorry I ever met you. ~~You lucky I put up with you for so long.~~ I can get anyone I want, *sabes*? You don't know what you got. I hope your moms and pops kicks you out again.

You got all these pipe dreams about being somebody but you never gonna be more than just a ghetto rat. You said we'd be together forever but you lied. So whatever. I don't need you.

You played me. And you gonna be sorry you ever played me like you did when I get out. That's a promise.

And that was just the beginning. Dio couldn't write fast enough. He must have written 10 pages by the time he was done. He was so pent up inside, he felt like he had to get it out. He sealed the envelope, put Jennifer's address, even put a stamp on it.

Maybe he should just mail it, he thought but he couldn't put it in the drop. The truth was he was scared. If he sent that letter, he'd never see her again.

"What are you doing?"

Dio jumped up. His heart jumped with him as he stood at attention, Jackson in front of his bunk.

"Ssss-sir. I . . . I was just . . ."

"Keeping your nose clean? What about your grades?"

"Sir, getting better, sir."

"Good, 'cause we don't let no dullards graduate. What's a *dullard*, trainee?"

"Sir, a dummy, sir."

Jackson smiled. "Good . . . good."

Dio's eyes followed Jackson as he paced back and forth, walking around him, examining him. It seemed like Jackson was missing him as much as he missed Jackson, but neither of them wanted to admit it.

He clenched the letter in his hands.

Writing it was a bad idea, he thought.

He needed to focus on getting out. If he did that, he'd tick Grossaint off in the best way – by succeeding. So when Jackson walked away, he went to the wastepaper basket brimming over with garbage and stuffed the letter on top.

Chapter 23

It was the Fourth of July and the officers had let some of the trainees go outside to watch the fireworks.

One of the good things about being so far from Vegas was that they could see all the fireworks pretty well. Dio's eyes lit up. With all before him, he couldn't help but wonder what Jennifer was doing.

So much had changed since the last Fourth of July.

All the flashes of red and blue brought Dio back to that awful rainy night, the last day he saw Jennifer, as they sped down the pothole-filled road from Vegas toward the L.A. highway.

They were finally going to leave their old life behind and start anew. It was their one chance to be together.

He was going to get out of the gang, he decided and she was going to go for her dream. They were running away, really. And though he thought about how Spooky would flip out if he found out what they were doing, he also knew that rival gangs were just waiting for a chance to catch him slipping. He needed out now.

He only hoped it wouldn't affect Jennifer. That's what motivated him to first start to pull away from the life. He wanted to be with her and if the only way was to leave the life, he was willing to do it.

He looked over at Jennifer, who was staring out the window, and reached for her hand.

"It's going to work out. We get to L.A., all our dreams will come true. You'll be near Hollywood and nobody knows me out there so we can start fresh. We're almost at the state line; nothing can stop us now."

That's when it happened.

Pop! Tss! The car swung sharply to the left and Dio realized they had a flat tire.

"What?!" He pulled over, slipping and sliding on the wet road. They both got out of the car and looked at the tire. The rain drenched them like wet dogs.

"This is bad," Jennifer said. "Real bad."

"We'll be fine. Promise. No matter what, *siempre.* Okay?" He smiled.

"*Siempre,*" she answered, though filled with doubt. Her eyes lit up as she saw a car's headlights off in the distance. "Look," she said, and she started waving them down.

Something bothered Dio. The approaching car's headlights dimmed and the car began to accelerate.

Dio could still remember the look of fright in Jennifer's eyes as she saw the guns blasting at them. He dove toward her to get her out of the way, but it was too late.

His past had caught up with them.

∞

Dio was making his way back to the others in the squad that Fourth of July night, when he noticed something moving near the trash bin.

It was some trainee, digging through it like a raccoon. He dropped a can of air freshener and stared at Dio, glassy-eyed.

Then he recognized him. It was Simon.

"Hey . . . hey, Dio. Good . . . good to see you, man," Simon said, his voice high and off.

"What are you doing?" Dio asked him approaching.

But Simon didn't need to answer. He'd known too many of his homies who did the same thing, getting high off aerosol cans.

"You know that stuff can mess you up," Dio said.

Simon grabbed him by the collar. "You won't tell, will you?"

Dio shoved him off. "'Course not. You only have a few months left here, *ése*. Why mess it up?"

Simon started laughing, then covered his face with his arm and started sobbing. Dio didn't know what to do.

"It's all right, man," Dio said.

Simon tried to suck up his tears. "Easy for you to say. You got a girl, you got a little brother, you got homies. I don't have anybody."

"You got your mom, eh?"

"She don't want me. My dad don't want me either. That's why I'm here. Cocaine, pot, whatever I could get my hands on. My parents got so fed up so.... they turned me in."

Dio sat down next to him. "Kind of a good thing, wasn't it?"

"It's my second time here, Dio. My parents gave up on me. That's why I was crying those first nights when you came. Sometimes, I just want to end it all."

"Whatchew talkin' about, foo'?" Dio shoved him in the shoulder.

"It was my fault you got knocked back," Simon confessed.

"*Chale,* homes, that wasn't your fault —"

"No, I wanted to get out so bad. I can't take this place no more. I ... It was me that made that hole in the wall, not Grossaint."

Dio reeled back, uneasy and upset. If it had been six months ago, he probably would have kicked Simon's butt. But now, he thought about things before he did them.

"Ever felt so locked up inside you want to go, but you can't get out? You go crazy inside, Dio. Crazy. "

Dio thought about all those years being locked in the toy box by his mother whenever he was "bad".

"*Chale,* homes. When we get out, you can crash at my pad with me and Jennifer. We're going to get jobs and go to college and . . . and every weekend, you and me and all my homies, gonna chill . . ."

Simon cracked a smile. "...with all the *jainas.*"

Dio laughed. "*Simón, ése.* And play oldies." He put his arm around Simon. "We're homies for life, *perro.* Homies *por vida.* Don't let those punks—"

"Yeah, dawg. They hit me, I got to hit 'em worse, right?" Simon interrupted.

Dio thought for a while, turned away and stared off into the distance.

And though later he'd regret saying it, he answered, "Yeah, sure."

Chapter 24

Dear Dio,

This is hard for me to say. The reason I haven't been feeling well or getting right back to you is because I found out something from the doctor months ago. I'm pregnant ~~with your baby~~.

Don't know if it's a boy or a girl. It's too soon to tell. I'm happy about this baby but now what am I supposed to do? They say the baby's due like October or November. I'm sorry you won't be out in time to see the birth but I'll send you pictures. OK?

Just ~~try to~~ be patient with me with the letters? OK? I want to see you too. There's things we need to talk about in person that I can't write about. Be good.

Jennifer

Dio could hardly contain himself. A father? They were going to be a real family. And they had a child, someone who would be testament to their love forever. It couldn't possibly be better news.

Chapter 25

Dear Jennifer,

I almost ~~shi~~ went in my pants when I got the news. You don't have to worry about nothing, porque as soon as I get out I'll work 2–3 jobs whatever it takes to support you and our baby. I'm going to be the best dad there is. Te lo prometo. I was thinking if it's a boy he could be Dio Jr. or Luis after my dad, and if it's a girl how about Jennifer, or Cristina?

I knew it was meant to be that we'd have a familia. See? I love you mija. And don't worry cause soon as I get out we can start planning the wedding too. I want to do it at the church on Valley View. You know the one we used to go to all the time when we were ~~kids~~ younger with Father Martínez? And you can invite all your relatives (even your mom. Ja-Ja-Ja.)

I don't care. I want ~~everyone~~ the world to know, nothing's going to break our love. Nothing. This is the best news ever!

Love,

Playboy aka Dio

Ever since Dio had gotten the news he had an extra bounce in his step. He told anyone who would listen about him becoming a daddy and even those who didn't want to listen.

Chapter 26

Another month had past and it was Visitor's Day again. Dio just wanted it over with so he could get back to the tent and dream up more plans for himself and Jennifer and their baby. It had been a long time since he'd heard from her but he figured she was going through a lot with the pregnancy and all. His only regret was that he wasn't by her side taking care of her.

Visitor's hour was almost over when he noticed a big girl, no, a pregnant girl waddling inside. Her hair was long and brown and . . . that's when Dio realized it was Jennifer.

He couldn't breathe. This had to be a fantasy. But it wasn't. She was really in the same room as he.

His whole face lit up at the sight of her. He had to restrain himself from running over to her.

She too lit up for a second. But then her face became more withdrawn; barely able to look at him. He took her by the hand and led her over to a bench, but she pulled it away.

He leaned over to kiss her but she turned away. He was hurt but something else was in her eyes, anger. It took awhile for either of them to say anything to each other. Neither knew where to start.

"I got your letter," she said.

Of course you got my letter; I sent it a month ago, Dio thought.

"Baby, I know I was a real *cabrón* before, but—"

"Don't 'baby' me."

Dio was shocked. He'd seen her angry before but not like that.

"What do you mean? *Que paso?*"

"*Que paso?*" she asked as if he should know already.

It had to be the hormones.

Jennifer started to speak when an officer said, "Time's up."

Dio could have shot him right then and there. Why'd she have to come so late? What was going on?

There was so much to say and now, so little time. Jennifer gathered her things together; more preoccupied with collecting her stuff than looking at him.

"Hey, Jennifer." He smiled.

She looked at him, her eyes fiery.

"No matter what—*siempre*. Eh?" he said.

She continued to gather her things.

"Do I at least get a hug?" he half-joked.

She looked him dead in the eye, shoved some papers into his chest hard, then she

69

stormed off as fast as any pregnant woman could.

"Jennifer!" he called after her until one of the junior officers gave him a dirty look. He tried to ignore the looks of the other trainees and their families.

He looked down at the folded and wrinkled papers and felt the color rush out of his face when he realized what they were.

The hate letter he thought he'd thrown it away. Someone must have found it and mailed it anyway. And in that moment he knew his world would never be the same again.

Chapter 27

When it finally hit Dio what had actually happened, it hit hard. He dropped to his knees, so sick he puked. He wanted to pray, but why? *What good would praying do if it resulted in this?*

He'd been praying day and night since he arrived in the camp for things to get better with him and Jennifer and now look what happened?

Half of Dio's squad was already out of the tent by the time he woke up. Outside, there was a monstrous racket. Dio stumbled outside and found himself facing three officers, struggling to keep Simon from screaming and fighting.

"I'll kill you!" he yelled.

For a moment, it almost seemed to Dio as if he were seeing his old-self being dragged away, long hair, punk-attitude. He had to rub his eyes. Was this really *Simon*?

The flashing red and blue lights reflected off him as they dragged him toward the patrol cars.

Simon caught one last sight of Dio as they lowered his head into the patrol car. Dio gestured for him to "chin up."

Simon's eyes watered.

Chapter 28

Dear Jennifer,

They booked Simon for attempted murder, on Grossaint. 25 years in the joint. Apparently he just snapped or something, and kept saying... well. Something I'd told him. I didn't mean it like that of course. They won't let him out until he's like 40 something years old. If he makes it that long. Spooky always said only the strong survive there and Simon will ~~never be that~~ always be a pussy cat.

I was so glad to see you. About the letter, please know, I never meant for you to see that. I was just heated that day. It was like a journal. You know I would never try to hurt you. We got to stay together 'cause I don't know what I'd do without you. I'ma be out of here sooner than you know and when I get out I'm going to get you a real ring, I promise whatever you want. I'm getting my GED next week. And everyone says I'm doing better. Just like I promised you I would change. We're going to work it out. Just wait for me, please.

Love,

Your Soulmate,

Dio

Louise dabbed her watery eyes. "I'm so sorry, about all of this."

He shrugged. "Used to it."

"But look how far you've come. Look at the man you've become." She smiled and touched his shoulder.

Dio nodded. He knew it was true, but he wanted more than that. He'd done all this for Jennifer and now it seemed it was all for nothing. "But . . ." he said, his voice cracking. "I want her."

He sobbed. Louise held him close and rubbed his back.

"I know, honey. I know."

He pulled back, wiped his tears with his sleeve, his nostrils flaring. "Well, I'm just going to have to show her I'm better than before. She'll see."

Louise searched for the right words. "Good."

Is that all she had to say?

He broke away from her and said, full of motivation, "She's going to see I'm much better than I ever was and I'm going to be successful and I'm going to be rich and I'm going to be the best husband and father she's ever seen."

Louise swallowed then looked away. "Good. That's wonderful."

"I am!" he announced. "You believe me, don't you?"

"I've got no doubt in my mind you can do that. It's just . . ."

"It's just what?"

She didn't know how to say it exactly, so she swallowed hard.

"Have you ever thought...? Sometimes you've got to love someone enough to think about their happiness, Dio. Maybe it's not meant to be like you thought; maybe it's okay to just let her go."

"What?" Dio asked, taking a breath and frowning. "You're the one who said I could win her back; that all I had to do was keep my nose clean, that's what you said."

"I know but—"

"Louise!"

"You want the truth, Dio? Sounds to me like she's just trying to get her life together," Louise said. "And good for her. What are you doing? How about trying to figure out how to get yourself together. Part of being a man is knowing when to let go. If you truly love her, maybe it's better to think about that. Maybe you should just let her go. It's gonna hurt but pain doesn't last forever."

The words were like a stab to the heart.

He grabbed the nearest thing he could find and threw it against the wall. "You lied to me. You're just like everyone else, full of it. This whole place is full of it. I hate your bull stories. I hate your bull advice. It don't mean nothing." He spat on the floor.

"Dio, I'm just trying to help," Louise said. She reached out to him, but he pulled away.

"You don't want to help. You're just some lonely housewife who needed someone to talk to," he spat.

Dio stormed toward the door, then stopped, turned to her, and said with a lump in his throat, "I'll send you pictures of us on our wedding day."

Chapter 29

"Radigez, get your butt over here and help me with this," Jackson said the next day, tinkering under the hood of his car. It was starting to get nippy again as the fall set in. Almost a year had passed since Dio had first stepped foot on the camp and he couldn't believe it.

"Sir, yes, sir!" Dio said, moving over. He was still thinking about the argument that he'd had with Louise and was starting to feel bad.

"I think it's the starter." Jackson said, clearing his throat. Then he cleared it again.

Oh great, Dio thought. He could tell Jackson wanted to say something. He only hoped it wouldn't be another long-winded lecture.

"So . . ." he started, clearing his throat again, "heard your girl stopped by."

"Sir, yes, sir." He didn't even want to think about the situation right now.

"Thought about how you're going to provide for the baby?" Jackson pressed.

Dio tried to keep his sigh undetected.

"Sir, who's ever going to hire Trainee Rodríguez with a conviction anyway, sir?"

"Well, that's not a good attitude." Jackson sat up and frowned. "How you ever going to own that car design shop you want to have one day if you. . .? 'Course . . . when I was about your age, had a couple of misdemeanors under my belt, too."

Dio looked at him, shocked. *Him?*

"Sir, misdemeanors?"

"Yeah." Jackson sniffed but didn't look up. "So I get it. I know what it's like."

"Sir," Dio said with a snort. "Everybody says they know what it's like and they don't. Never had a decent mother. Been in and out of juvie since I was thirteen. Don't got no money. Don't got no car. Don't even got no lady no more. How do you think I'm supposed to get a decent job if I—?"

Jackson slammed the hood of the car shut and stepped nose-to-nose with Dio. "No, no and no! You think you had it hard. Well, boo-hoo, Radigez. You know what it's like to wake up three o'clock every morning to pick strawberries with your alcoholic stepfather? "

"Sir, no sir," Dio answered.

"Well, Trainee Franklin does. You know what it's like to be a rape baby, your mother using you like a human ironing board every day 'cause she hates the Mexican that did it to her and she hates you 'cause you remind her of it?"

"Sir, no, sir."

"Well, Grossaint does."

Dio blinked. *Grossaint was half Mexican?*

"You know what it's like to go to work every day, facing the same type of gang-banging loser thugs that killed your son?" Jackson continued. "Every day hoping that you might make a difference in their pathetic little lives? Huh?"

Jackson's eyes were watery, his lips quivering.

"Sir ... no sir," Dio didn't know what to do. He'd never seen Jackson cry before. In fact, he'd never seen a grown man cry before.

"Well, I . . . I do," he said, trying to cough away the tears. "So, boo-hoo, boo-hoo, Radigez. 'Cause everybody's got a story."

He took a handkerchief out and blew his nose loudly, then coughed some more. "Think about what I could have done every day to prevent it. Maybe kept him from the wrong crowd, been there for him 'stead of the office all the time. But there are no excuses in life, Radigez. That's one thing I know."

He fished his pockets for a cigarette, and then took a puff. "Sit down."

"Sir, yes, sir."

Dio sat on top of a rock as Jackson cooled off, pacing back and forth.

"You're scared, aren't you, Trainee?"

Dio thought for a while. "Sir, yes, sir. Trainee Rodríguez don't know exactly how he's going to be a good father, not sure if he can handle it."

"Well, Radigez, I was scared, too. Every new father is. But I tell you one thing, being a dad's probably going to be the best thing that's ever happened to you. Was for me."

Dio looked at Jackson, and for the first time, saw the human behind the shell.

"Truth is, sometimes you remind me of him, hardheaded son of a gun," Jackson said, stamping out his cigarette. Then he tossed Dio a package. "Happy birthday."

Dio's eyes about popped out when he opened the package and found a uniform. All white, the last level.

"Don't ever say I never gave you nothing," Jackson grunted, fighting back a smile.

"Sir, yes, sir!"

"Go on now, get over to your squad. And don't you never give up on that girl of yours."

"Sir, yes, sir."

Dio got up to leave, but Jackson stopped him. "And Radigez? Don't you tell nobody 'bout me crying, neither, or I'll kick your butt."

Dio grinned from ear to ear. "Sir, yes, sir."

He couldn't get to the hooch fast enough. He only wished Jennifer could share his happiness.

Chapter 30

Months passed. Winter crept in before they realized and soon it was Christmas. Dio had just about given up hope on ever getting Jennifer back or hearing from her and though he continued to progress with the squad, there wasn't a night he didn't go to sleep thinking about her.

He'd been working diligently in the camp to become the best man he could be; studying harder, pushing harder -- whatever it took. But still, there was part of him that wondered if it would be enough.

All he could do was pray.

It was unusually quiet in the hooch as Jackson passed out the Christmas mail to the trainees. Seemed like everyone got a card or gift, except Dio and Grossaint who was all patched up and had a nasty scar across his throat from Simon's attack. Dio almost felt sorry for him.

"Radigez!" Jackson called, tossing him a letter. Dio looked at it with surprise. It was from Jennifer.

"Sir, thank you, sir," he said, trying to contain his excitement.

Jackson smiled.

Dio ripped open the envelope. He wouldn't miss this for the world. It still smelled like her perfume. He pulled the letter out and a little pocket picture popped out. A picture of a beautiful baby girl and a Rolos chocolate. Dio smiled with pride.

Merry Christmas Dio,

I know it's been a long time since we talked. But I wanted you to know that our baby ~~are~~ is fine. She was born on November 11th. Her name is Crystal Dione Rodríguez. The Dio part in Dione is for you. She was 7 pounds 4 ounces and she's got your ~~brown~~ eyes. Ojos sonrientes we call her.

For the longest time I was just angry. Not just about the letter but at some of the choices I've made in my past.

I know you have graduation coming up and wanted to say I'm so proud of you.

Life changes everything. Time goes by and people change, what we want in our life changes. We become different people no matter how much we tried to hold on to the past. I guess what I'm trying to say is just like my ~~boy~~ friend Angel says, "Sometimes you've just got to –

Rip!

Before Dio could react, Grossaint grabbed his letter and picture and ripped them to shreds.

"Figured we needed some Christmas decorations." Grossaint chuckled, tossing the pieces in the air.

Everyone froze, wondering what Dio would do next.

Dio's lips got tighter. He stormed over to Grossaint, fuming, tapped him on the shoulder and handed him the Rolos Jennifer sent him.

"Merry Christmas," Dio said, and he walked away.

Grossaint, stunned, opened his hand and looked at the chocolate like it was the best gift he had ever received. He even started to tear up.

Was Dio furious? Of course. But for some reason, he actually felt more sorry for Grossaint than anything. If he felt so bad about himself that he needed to ruin someone's Christmas, he really had to be messed up in the head. Besides, as Louise used to say, it was only a matter of time before karma hit him.

"Officer on deck!" someone yelled.

Grossaint looked up as Jackson got in his face.

"What is going on here, Grossaint?" Jackson yelled.

"I . . . I . . ."

"Destroying personal property, Grossaint?"

"Sir, I . . . I . . . didn't do nothing."

"Sir, I specifically saw Trainee Grossaint tearing up Trainee Radigez's personal property," Grossaint's friend Franklin said.

One by one, everyone in the squad repeated the same.

"Me too," they each said.

"Shut up," Grossaint snapped.

"I'll do the shutting up around here, Grossaint," Jackson said, grabbing him by the collar.

Chapter 31

It was only days before graduation and Dio knew there was one last thing he had to do. He cleared his throat, stepping behind Louise in the kitchen.

She looked at Dio, then went back to putting the canned foods away.

"How was your Christmas?" Dio asked, trying to break the ice.

"You're a little late," she grumbled.

Dio cleared his throat. "Graduation's coming up."

"Uh-huh," she said.

"Look, I know sometimes I haven't been the easiest to be around-" he started.

"No?" she said, raising her eyebrows.

"No." He cracked a smile, "But you've really helped me a lot when other people wouldn't have given me a shot and . . ." He scratched his foot on the floor. "That was real cool of you."

"Is that your way of apologizing?" she asked, turning around to face him.

He blushed. "Sorry... gonna miss you," he said.

"Gonna miss you, too." She hugged him tight. "You can contact me any time. I'm in the phone book."

"Thanks. I . . . better get going," he said, backing away.

"Yeah, you better," she teased, her eyes becoming watery.

He stopped, turned around and asked, "Louise?"

"What, kiddo?" she asked.

"Can I call you 'Mom'?" he asked biting the inside of his mouth.

She couldn't help herself, a lone tear trailed down her cheek, "Sure."

Chapter 33

It was a little nippy that graduation day, but the sun was bright. Dio stood proudly onstage, looking pretty snazzy in his graduation uniform with the other graduates-to-be.

"Been a long time coming for these trainees," Jackson said from the podium. "Colorful backgrounds, but they've come a long way. A lot farther than many of them ever believed they could."

He put his speech cards away and looked at them all with a sparkle in his eyes. "Had a whole speech prepared but ... to tell you the truth, no words can describe how hard these trainees have worked to get where they are. Some of them have come from real tough backgrounds. They had every reason in the world not to be standing here today. But they made it. Somehow, they made it. These boys, these men, probably have more fighting spirit than I've ever seen."

Dio had to admit, he was happier than he'd been in years. Still, he was distracted, looking for Jennifer in the crowd.

She had to be there somewhere. Even after he received his graduation certificate, he searched the crowd all around the ground but she was nowhere to be seen.

Someone tugged at his sleeve.

"Dio?"

It was his little brother, Daniel.

Dio scooped his brother up without a thought, his throat tight and chills running through his body. He couldn't believe it.

"What are you doing here?" he asked.

"*Mami's* here."

Dio set Daniel down and his eyes met his mother's.

She didn't look like the drunken mess he remembered. She'd cleaned up. Now she moved slowly up to him, her eyes begging for his forgiveness.

They didn't say a word, either of them, just hugged.

"This your mom?" Dio heard Jackson say as he approached them.

"Nice to meet you," she said.

"Likewise. You oughta be proud of this boy of yours. I know I am."

Dio didn't know what to say, Jackson had never said anything like that to him.

His mom pulled Daniel away so that he and Jackson could have some privacy.

"Where's your girl? I was hoping to meet her." Jackson asked.

"Um . . . I don't know. Maybe stuck in traffic," Dio said, hoping it was true.

"Well . . . look. Wanted to give you this."

He took out a business card and passed it to Dio. The card read, JO'S CAR DESIGN SHOP.

"Friend of the family. Told her about you and . . . well, you'll probably have to start out sweeping the floors, but—"

Dio couldn't contain himself. He hugged Senior Jackson tightly, then pulled back, embarrassed.

Jackson blushed, though he tried to hide his smile.

"Well . . . just don't go and blow it. I put my name on the line for you."

"Sir, yes, sir," Dio smiled.

"Well . . . You keep your nose clean, you hear?"

"Sir, yes, sir."

"Ever need anything, just pick up the phone and..."

"I'll miss you, too, sir," Dio said.

Jackson cleared his throat and tried to hide his smile, then mumbled something to the effect of, "I'm proud of ya'."

Dio smiled then spent the next hour or so saying good-bye to his fellow graduating trainees, looking around for Jennifer. She never came.

Chapter 35

Months more passed. He looked everywhere for Jennifer, even called every old number he had for her, but they were disconnected.

Someone said she moved but nobody knew where. It seemed like she'd completely disconnected from everyone in the old barrio.

Dio too didn't want to step foot back in his old barrio nor did he want a reminder of who he used to be. He just wanted to leave the past behind. But he knew if there was one person that knew where Jennifer was, it had to be his homie, Spooky.

"Look at you," Spooky said, falling out of his chair as he looked at Dio for the first time in over a year.

Beer bottles and old pizza boxes littered Spooky's living room. Two or three of his women were knocked out from a night of partying.

Spooky got up and walked around Dio like he was checking out a brand-new car.

"That you, Playboy?" he joked.

"Call me Dio, bro."

"Dio?" Spooky laughed, "A'ight, Dio. When'd you get out, dawg?"

"Few weeks ago. Got a job."

Spooky almost choked on his beer, "Job? For real?"

"Yep, at an auto shop on Decatur. Only seven dollars an hour, but might end up being assistant manager soon."

"Assistant manager?" Spooky laughed. "You?"

They paused. The silence between them made Dio realize he really didn't have much to talk to Spooky about anymore. He was so much different now. He wanted different things and for the first time in his life, he liked who he was becoming.

He looked around.

"Where's Little Spider?"

Spooky cleared his throat. "Got shot last month... Didn't make it."

Dio could barely speak. His hands got sweaty and his throat dry. He'd known Spider since he was in junior high.

"What about Bullet and Trix?" he asked.

"Got locked up four months ago. Trix OD'd just after you got busted. Yeah, *ése.* Hard times. Hard times."

It was like his whole former world had come crashing down. He couldn't help but think that could have been him. Maybe being in boot camp was the best thing to have happened to him after all.

"Why you all dressed up today, anyway? You going to church or something?" Spooky asked, changing the subject.

"No," Dio said, collecting his thoughts. He pulled a little box out of his pocket and opened it to reveal a beautiful diamond engagement ring. He finally bought the ring he'd always promised Jennifer he'd get her.

"Where'd you swipe that from?" Spooky said.

"Didn't. Bought it."

"Bought it?" Spooky looked as if that was the shock of the century.

"Gonna check around Jennifer's old stomping grounds to propose. You seen her?"

Spooky turned pale. "No one told you?"

"What?" Dio asked.

"*Ese*, Jennifer . . . she . . . she got engaged to this foo' a couple of months ago."

It was as if someone had taken a hammer to Dio's head. He had to keep his knees from buckling and dropping to the floor.

"Engaged? Who'd she --?" Dio asked.

"Some *pinche negro*. Supposed to get married this weekend. Thought you knew."

Chapter 36

Now the moment was here.

"Don't be stupid foo'," Spooky said, grabbing hold of Dio in his car.

"Just keep the car runnin', *ése*," Dio answered, jumping out of the car in the pouring rain.

Dio's heart raced as he sat in the chapel, reaching for the .45 caliber in his jacket pocket. He could hear the rain pounding against the stained glass windows and the roof. He crossed himself, closed his eyes, and prayed he was about to do the right thing.

Boom! Thunder rumbled and Dio jumped as the lights went out.

"Waaaaaaaaah!"

Everyone stopped. A baby was crying.

It was Dio's baby, lying in Jennifer's mom's arms. When her crying wouldn't stop, her mom rocked her. It was the first time Dio had laid eyes on his daughter and it did something to him. Her cry was a wake-up call.

How could he even think it?

Dio got up and snuck through the crowd to the back of the cathedral.

Baby Crystal kept screaming, no matter how many times the priest tried to wrap up the ceremony. Finally, Jennifer turned to grab her.

"I'm so sorry," she said, sweeping Crystal away down the aisle. She ran into Dio just as he was about to step out the door.

They both froze. Then Dio collected himself.

"Congratulations," he swallowed, not sure what to say exactly.

"Thanks," she responded. She looked down at Crystal, who stopped crying, and smiled. "Say 'hello' to your daddy, *mija.*"

She handed her to Dio.

Crystal was so small that Dio was almost afraid to hold her, but he did and couldn't help the tears that welled.

"Hi, *mija.* I'm your daddy."

He let her little fingers grab hold of his pinky as he played with her little pouty lips. He smiled and Jennifer smiled back.

"You're a natural, daddy," she said.

He cleared his throat and looked at Jennifer. "Anything you need, I'll be here. I want to be a good dad."

"You will be," she said.

They looked at each other for a moment, their eyes full of a kind of love, but then, from outside, came the honk of a car horn. Spooky.

"I better go," Dio said, breaking away from the moment.

"Yeah, me too," Jennifer replied. "Kind of in the middle of something."

He handed Crystal back, started to kiss Jennifer goodbye, but instead kissed her on the cheek.

"See ya," he said.

"Yeah." Jennifer sniffed, her face crumpling.

He started for the door again, then winked. "No matter what—*siempre,* eh?"

She smiled, tears welling up in her eyes. "Yeah. Forever."

NOTE FROM THE AUTHOR:

Dear Readers,
Should there be a sequel to *No Matter What?*

Email me at Jeff@JeffRivera.com to let me know. If I get enough requests, I'll write the sequel. If not, maybe I'll write something different.

The choice is yours.

--Jeff Rivera

CPSIA information can be obtained at www.ICGtesting.com
Printed in the USA
LVOW05s1357210314

378414LV00011B/86/P